Marilynne K. Roach

The Mouse and the Song

illustrated by J O S E P H L O W

Parents' Magazine Press

New York

For my parents

Text Copyright © 1974 by Marilynne Roach
Illustrations Copyright © 1974 by Joseph Low
Printed in the United States of America

Library of Congress Cataloging in Publication Data

Roach, Marilynne K.
  The mouse and the song.
  SUMMARY: A little mouse becomes friendly with the
lone man living at Walden Pond.
  Bibliography: p.
  [1. Mice—Fiction. 2. Thoreau, Henry David, 1817-
1862. Walden—Fiction] I. Low, Joseph, 1911-
illus. II. Title.
PZ7.R528Mo   [E]   73-13877
ISBN 0-8193-0721-1   ISBN 0-8193-0722-X (lib. bdg.)

AUTHOR'S NOTE

Most of this story is based on fact. The man is Henry David Thoreau who, from 1845-7, lived in a small cabin he built on the shore of Walden Pond a mile and a half from the village of Concord, Massachusetts. In Walden, *Thoreau wrote of the mouse who lived in his cellar and who shared his lunches. Memoirs by his friends recall that the mouse loved hearing Thoreau's flute music. A note penciled in the margin of his* Journal *reveals that the mouse was female.*

As for Mouse's singing, that is not mentioned. But mice do sing—only rarely, but they do.

There was a certain white-footed mouse who lived in the woods by a pond, and to her, life was a constant searching for the seeds, berries, bark and insects that mice eat.

But other hungry, harried animals eat mice. So life was
also running from the fox, the weasel and the silent owl.

Life was establishing a territory large enough to provide food, and then defending it against other mice. Life was making a shelter to live in out of the cold and wet.
Life was scurrying through mazes of paths in summer grasses to catch crickets. And darting over snowfields in winter when there was not much cover.
And important also, life was finding a mate and raising young, for mice are the prey of many and only their numbers save them. That is the way of mice.

Once in summer, Mouse claimed a territory in a clearing where a man was building a cabin. It seemed a likely place to live. Already a phoebe had her nest in the woodshed and a robin family lived in a nearby pine. Rabbits and raccoons moved like shadows about the dooryard at evening and an occasional woodchuck would amble past through the scrub oak and sumac.

Wind blew through the trees from across the nearby pond
bringing the scents and sounds of passing animals. And
there was sometimes a strange sound also, a clear singing
such as no bird made. But it was not a threat, so Mouse
built a snug nest of grass and wood-shavings in the sandy
cellar of the cabin and there bore her young.

For two whole days while the man went about his work outside and in the room above, Mouse tended to her babies.
She hummed a buzzing song as white-footed mice sometimes
do, and never left them, not even to eat or drink. By the
third day, when they could be safely left alone for a while,
Mouse went out to look for food.

Mouse now saw her first human being. He was
sitting outside against the wall eating his noon lunch
when she came from the cellar. Crumbs of bread and cheese
had fallen at his feet. Since this new animal did not
seem like a threat to Mouse, she dashed forward, snatched
several crumbs in her mouth and ran back to the cellar.

The man didn't do anything to stop her, so she went the next day for more crumbs and soon made a habit of joining him for lunch.

One day, Mouse ran up the cabin wall and clung to the rough boards a moment to get a better look at the man. Then she jumped to his shoulder and ran down his sleeve to his hand.

She sat there eating a piece of cheese from his fingers.
His palm smelt of pine resin from the wood he had been
handling that day. When she finished, Mouse hopped down,
washed her face and paws and calmly walked away.

Soon they were making a game of lunch. The man would pretend to hide crumbs in his hand while Mouse ran along his arm and round and round, dodging and pouncing until he gave her the cheese.

She always ate it neatly and wiped her face and paws like
a fly before she left him.

Mouse's life was still very busy though. Her babies became more and more active as they grew. She had to nurse them and still find enough food to keep up her own strength.

And when she went out after seeds and fruits she had to be
wary of the foxes that sometimes came around the clearing
or of the hawks that fell out of the sky and pounced
before their victims knew anything was going to happen.

Soon the man moved into his cabin full time. Other people came by to visit, though Mouse generally avoided them. Some would talk with the man by the hour, going on and on. Only the chattering red squirrels could give them any competition, or the whip-poor-will that sat on the ridgepole every evening to repeat and repeat his whistling call.

But when the man was alone as he usually was, and not working on the cabin, or in the garden, or walking off somewhere, he spent his time in two ways. He would sit quietly outdoors just looking and feeling, or he would write, turning his thoughts and feelings into words.

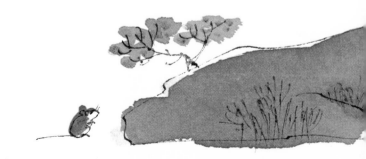

And Mouse heard the strange singing more often now,
but she did not know yet what caused it.
One night when Mouse crept back to her nest,
she heard the singing coming through the floor above.
She paused to listen. It wasn't exactly like a bird
but what else could sound like that? Quickly
she scrambled up the wall and squeezed out into the room
of the cabin. The man was sitting in the rocking chair
holding a long wooden tube. He blew across a hole near
one end of it while working his fingers over other holes
along its length to make the sweet sounds.

Mouse held perfectly still listening and listening. She
was lost in the music and filled with it as with breath, so
that she did not know when it had entered into her and
she into it.

A trill of high notes fell in that small room like bright
rain, followed by a lower passage that ran like streams
under the earth. The flute sang clustering sounds, bright
as sun sparkles on moving water, and single notes that
struck the air with the sharpness of winter stars.

When the man had finished the song he smiled to see
Mouse watching him. But Mouse flicked back into the
cellar and down to her nest where she lay for a long
while as the man continued to play upstairs. Then she
went outside to finish her night's work of foraging.

On the next night when the man played the flute she went
back. Night after night she came to listen until the
music became a part of her life, a part not concerned
with running away or being hungry. Hearing the music
was like eating a juicy bud after a winter of dry withered
hulls. Soon Mouse was sitting on the man's shoulder as
he played, to be near the vibrating flute.

The fox, the owl, the weasel, the hawk were still a part
of Mouse's days and nights, but now she had the music as
well and it could not be taken from her.

Mouse's babies grew up. When they began finding food for themselves and their fur changed from gray to an adult rust, they went off on their own.

Now with only herself to care for, Mouse began gathering nuts and seeds for the winter.

The man, too, prepared for colder weather by finishing the cabin. He had to shingle and plaster the walls, install a hearth, and lay a second floor over the single layer of rough boards then in place. But first he cleaned the cellar.

And when Mouse came home, the dust, the shavings and all
her hidden nest were swept away. Confused, she ran out of
the cellar, dodged across the clearing from cover to cover
and streaked up a chestnut tree. From high in its branches
Mouse looked down and saw the man going into the cabin
with a bucket of water.

Suddenly, some branches above her, a red squirrel began
buzzing a warning. Mouse turned to look, and there, gliding
down the branch, head low, eyes fixed upon her, was a mink.

With a squeak of alarm, Mouse scrabbled to the end of the
branch and leapt for the nearest twig. The mink ran close
behind as she dodged and twisted. They ran from tree to
tree until Mouse slipped and fell, thrashing through twigs,
grabbing at leaves.

She caught her balance finally on a low-hanging limb and,
spying a small hole in a rotten branch, hid inside.

Her fall startled a pair of blue jays who now saw the mink
and flew up screeching at the intruder. The mink had lost
Mouse's scent, so he turned and flowed away along the upper
branches with the noisy birds following.

Mouse stayed in the hole until the following evening
and when she came out she had no idea where she was
or where the clearing was. The clean scent of water
blew from the nearby pond, and passing ducks
called to each other high in the air.

So Mouse made a new territory in the woods, small but good
enough, and built a home in an abandoned bird's nest in
a scrub oak. She roofed it over with dried grass and lined
it with chewed-up bits of feathers and moss.
Mouse was more cautious than ever in her new life away
from the cabin. She stored seeds and nuts against the
winter in the crack of a nearby stump. She hid from the
predators and studied each warning breeze.
Sometimes she thought she heard the flute again, very faint
and distant, but was never sure where the sound came from.
Her life in the cabin seemed long ago and far away, hardly
real anymore. She was almost never reminded of it.

But there was one gray dawn when the hollow clamor of migrating geese came ringing from the sky. The north was dark with advancing snow clouds, and everything down to the last grass blade was edged with white frost.

Mouse sat in the spiny tangle of a barberry bush eating
one of its bright red fruits. When she finished, she wiped
her paws and face and sat looking at the sky. It was empty
for the moment except for hurrying clouds. The breeze
brought no dangerous scents.

Then Mouse sang. She tipped back her head and sang in a
high, clear trill like the trilling of some small bird.

This was not the insect-buzzing she had sometimes hummed
before, but a true song that rang like silver in the cold
morning air. She clung to the thorns and sang from the
center of her being.

When she had done, she climbed down from the bush and
returned to her nest as the first flakes of winter snow came
drifting down.

Marilynne K. Roach grew up in Watertown, Massachusetts.
She graduated from the Massachusetts College of Art and
‎lustrator. When she first read
‎ken with the mouse episode,
‎hen she saw the tracks of just
‎en Woods by the Andromeda
‎ story in it.

‎and illustrator of many well-
‎ is also the founder of Eden
‎rints from Eden Hill, as well
‎paintings by him, have been
‎ver the world. For Parents'
‎ illustrated *Stargazer to the
‎Willow Plate*.